SIMON & SCHUSTER BOOKS FOR YOUNG READERS
An imprint of Simon & Schuster Children's Publishing Division
1230 Avenue of the Americas, New York, New York 10020

For information about special discounts for bulk purchases, please contact
Simon & Schuster Special Sales at 1-866-506-1949 or business@simonandschuster.com.
The Simon & Schuster Speakers Bureau can bring authors to your live event.
For more information or to book an event contact the Simon & Schuster Speakers Bureau
at 1-866-248-3049 or visit our website at www.simonspeakers.com.
Book design by Chloe Foglia, based on a design by Einav Aviram
The text for this book is set in Coop Light and Mister Sirloin.
The illustrations for this book are rendered
using Winsor and Newton oil paints on cotton canvas.
Manufactured in China · 0411 SCP
10 9 8 7 6 5 4 3 2 1
Library of Congress Cataloging-in-Publication Data
Meadows, Michelle.
Traffic pups / Michelle Meadows ; illustrated
by Dan Andreasen.-1st ed.
p. cm.
Summary: Canine motorcycle police officers zoom through the town
pursuing suspects, clearing the road of accidents, and serving as
escorts.
ISBN 978-1-4169-2485-2 (hardcover)
[1. Motorcycle police-Fiction. 2. Police-Fiction. 3. Dogs-Fiction.
4. Stories in rhyme.] I. Andreasen, Dan, ill. II. Title.
PZ8.3.M4625Bik 2009
[E]-dc22
2007037882

For my husband, Richard,
with love-M. M.

For Emily-D. A.

Acknowledgments
Special thanks to Rosemary Stimola
for putting the pups on the road.-M. M.

TRAFFIC PUPS

By MICHELLE MEADOWS

Illustrated by DAN ANDREASEN

Simon & Schuster Books for Young Readers

NEW YORK   LONDON   TORONTO   SYDNEY

Fasten helmets.
Rev it up.
Through the city . . .

Rip and rumble
down the street.
Silver badges—
on the beat.

Two cars speeding,
racing fast.

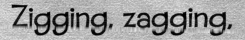

Zigging, zagging,

AT FULL BLAST!

Flip the sirens.
Hit a bump!
Hold on tight and

JUMP, JUMP, JUMP!

Zooming, vrooming,

UP, UP, UP!

Perfect landing . . .

TRAFFIC PUPS!

Tickets for a
mouse and toad.

Hop back on and
hit the road!

Red-light runner
on the loose.
Captain Dog says,

"CATCH THAT GOOSE!"

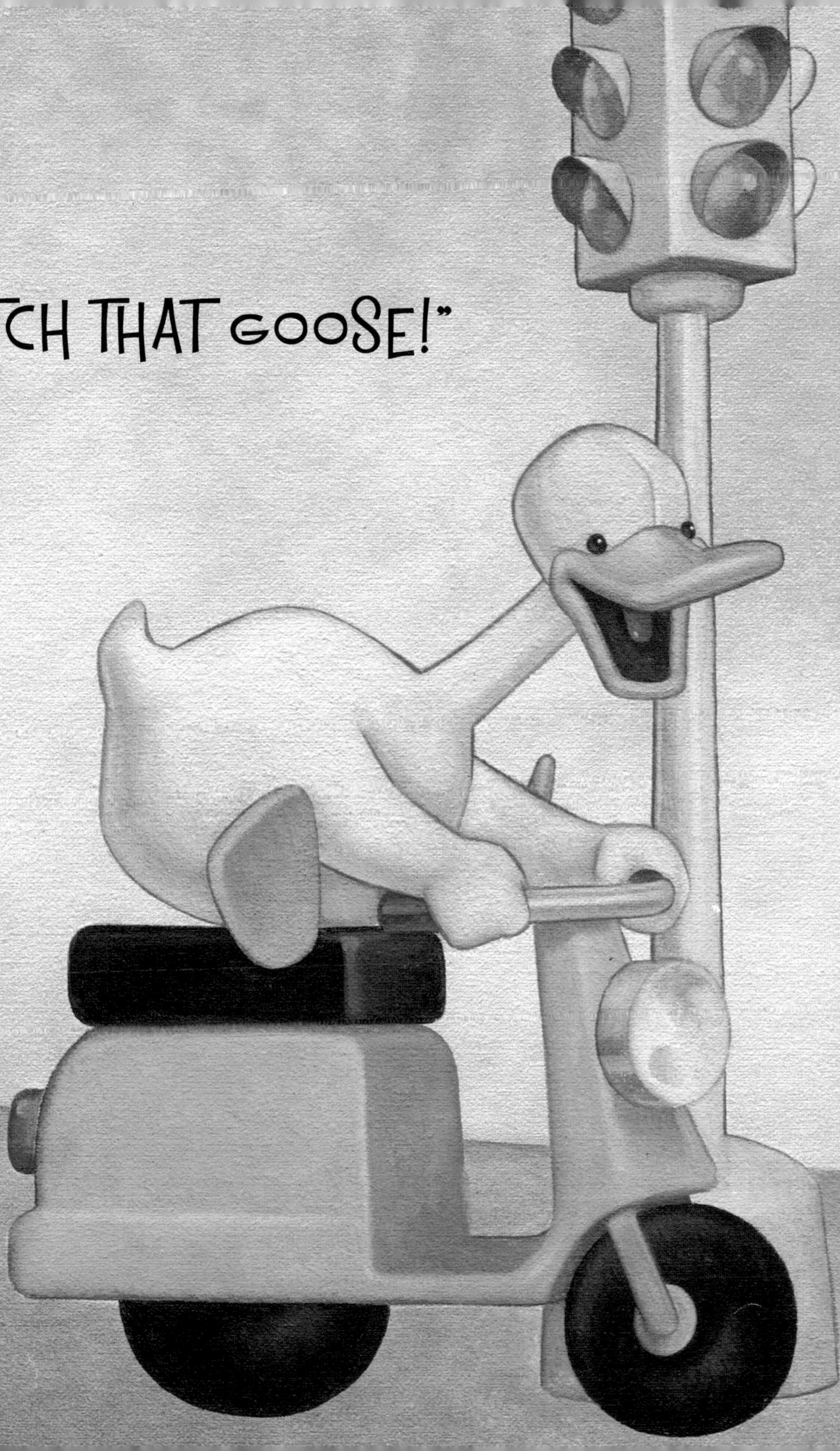

On the shoulder,
license check.

Called off to a
highway wreck.

Take the off-ramp,
pull on up.
To the rescue . . .

TRAFFIC PUPS!

Clear the roadway.
Truckers tow.
Pups direct the
traffic flow.

See the drivers lining up.
Look who's leading . . .

TRAFFIC PUPS!

To the station—
RACE. RACE. RACE!

Pull into a
parking space.

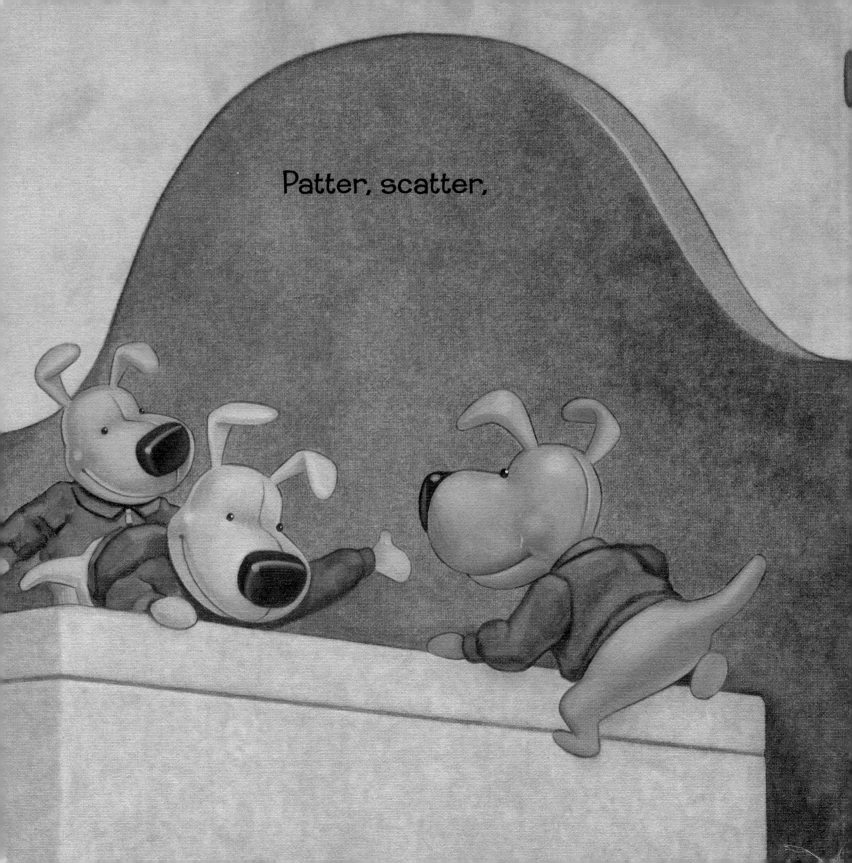

Patter, scatter,

in position.

Ready for the
next big mission.